LAMB LESSONS

Books in the Animal Ark Pets series

BEN M. BAGLIO

LAMB LESSONS

**Illustrated by
Paul Howard**

**Cover Illustration by
Chris Chapman**

*6 BOOKS so I havet
to get (5) more
for it to Be
all, 11*

A
LITTLE APPLE
PAPERBACK

SCHOLASTIC INC.

New York Toronto London Auckland Sydney
Mexico City New Delhi Hong Kong

ISBN 0-439-05168-1

12 11 10 9 8 7 6 5

1 2 3 4 5/0

40

Printed in the U.S.A.

First Scholastic Trade printing, June 2000

Special thanks to Pat Posner

Contents

LAMB LESSONS

1

A Bit of a Bully

"I'm glad Mrs. Todd didn't put *me* with Dillon for our project," said Jill Redfern when she and Mandy Hope came out of Welford Elementary School. "Look at him, bossing poor Samantha around."

Mandy glanced over to see Dillon Lewis steering his younger sister back toward the building. Mandy made a face as she heard him say, "You know you have to bring your lunch box home! Go get it, Samantha. And be quick or I'll go without you, and then you'll be in trouble for being late!"

"It must be worse for Samantha," Mandy said. "She has to live with him! At least we only have to put up with him at school. And," she added with a sigh, "we can keep out of his way most of the time."

"Maybe he'll forget to ask his mom to sign the permission slip from Mrs. Todd," said Jill. "If he doesn't bring it back on Monday, he won't be able to come to the farm with us."

"Well, I won't forget to get my letter signed," said Mandy, starting to hurry across the playground. "I'm going to try to forget about Dillon for a while. There's my mom. She's taking me to visit James."

James Hunter, Mandy's best friend, had gone into Welford Hospital the day before to have his tonsils out. He was only staying there for a couple of days. He was going home tomorrow, but Mandy had promised she'd visit.

"See you Monday, Jill," said Mandy as she opened the passenger door of her mom's car.

"Don't forget your boots!" Jill said. "And say hello to James."

"Boots?" Dr. Emily Hope asked.

Mandy nodded. "Our class is going to Woodbridge Farm Park for three mornings next week," she explained as she fastened her seat belt. "It's for a project we're doing on farm animals."

"I know someone who'll enjoy that!" Dr. Emily smiled, glancing at Mandy before they drove off.

"We'll be working in pairs," Mandy told her mom. "Each pair is going to learn how to take care of a different animal. We'll find out as much as we can about it and make notes and draw pictures to put in a special project book when we get back to school."

"Which animal will you be learning about?" asked Dr. Emily.

"I don't know yet," Mandy replied. "Mrs. Todd will tell us when we get to the farm on Monday morning."

Mandy frowned a little as she thought about being paired with Dillon Lewis.

"You don't seem very excited about it, Mandy." Dr. Emily was puzzled. She and Mandy's dad were both vets. Their clinic, Animal Ark, was down a street off Welford Village's Main Street. It was attached to the old stone cottage where they lived. Mandy loved animals and couldn't wait for the day when she'd be old enough to help her parents in the clinic. Usually, anything at all to do with animals made her talk nonstop.

"You're not worried about visiting James in the hospital, are you?" Dr. Emily asked gently.

Mandy shook her head. "It's not that," she said. "Mrs. Hunter said James was fine when I phoned her last night. It's just that . . . Mrs. Todd has paired me with Dillon Lewis!" she burst out. "He's horrible, Mom! He's small, but he's a real bully. Some of my friends are scared of him. I'm not scared. I just don't like him."

"Oh, dear," Dr. Emily said.

They were driving past the village green toward the road to Walton. The hospital was about a mile down the road.

"Well," Mandy's mom continued, "nobody's all bad. Maybe Mrs. Todd paired you with Dillon because she thinks you can bring out the best in him. And he might act completely differently with animals. Some people do, you know. In fact, there's a good example right now — over by the big oak tree."

Mandy looked over to see Mrs. Ponsonby. She was carrying Pandora, her overweight Pekingese, and talking to a man cutting the grass on the green. She seemed to be talking loudly and kept pointing at the longer grass around the oak tree.

Although Mrs. Ponsonby lived on the outskirts of the village in a huge old house called Bleakfell Hall, she tried to take charge of whatever was going on in the village itself, and she could be very bossy. Today, it looked as if she was ordering the workman to cut the grass shorter. But for all her bossy ways, Mrs. Ponsonby was really gentle and silly with Pandora.

"Though, of course, she spoils Pandora," Dr. Emily continued. "She feeds her too many treats and doesn't seem to realize it would do Pandora good to walk!"

Maybe Dillon will act differently while we're at the farm, Mandy thought. She smiled at her mother. "I *am* excited about going!" she said. "And James will be really interested when I tell him about it." James was eight, a year younger than Mandy. He was in Mrs. Black's class.

Dr. Emily smiled back as she turned into the gravel drive that led up to the small hospital. It was a long, low building with a flower garden in front and green shutters.

"There's James, looking out of the window!" said Mandy. "You remembered to bring his present, didn't you, Mom?"

Dr. Emily pointed to the glove compartment. Mandy opened it and pulled out a neatly wrapped parcel. It was a book she and her mom had bought at the school book fair. On the cover was a picture of a black Labrador puppy exactly like Blackie, James's puppy. As soon as Mandy had seen it, she'd known it was perfect for James.

Mandy jumped out of the car and waved to her friend. "He sees us, Mom!"

The children's ward was on the ground floor. The big swinging doors that led to the ward were covered with pictures of toys and animals. The ward itself was bright and cheerful-looking. The ten beds, five against each wall, were all covered with boldly colored bedspreads.

As Mandy and Dr. Emily entered the ward, James appeared from the playroom on the left and called to them to come in.

"How do you feel, James? You look okay," said Mandy.

"My throat's a little sore," he replied, "but I'll be going home tomorrow. It's great in here,

8

though." And as he unwrapped the present Mandy handed him, he told her and Dr. Emily that he'd had three bowls of ice cream already that day!

"Wow," he said, gazing down at his book. "This looks great, Mandy. Thank you."

Mandy grinned and told him all the news from school.

"Maybe you'll get Dillon for your animal," said James. Dillon was a duckling he and Mandy had taken to live at Woodbridge Farm Park.

"Oh, no!" said Mandy. "I don't think that would go over well with Dillon Lewis. He'd say Mrs. Todd did it on purpose because they have the same name! And then he'd be *really* awful to work with!"

"Samantha says Dillon's okay when there's just the two of them," James said. Dillon's sister was in the same class as James. "She says he only acts tough when there are other kids around. That way they won't tease him like their older brothers do at home."

Mandy looked thoughtful. "Well, maybe he'll be all right when we're alone with the animal we'll be learning about," she said.

After Mandy and James talked a while longer, Dr. Emily said it was time to go. "Clinic hours at Animal Ark start soon," she said, glancing at her watch.

Mandy said she'd visit James at home after school one day next week to tell him all about Woodbridge Farm Park.

She felt happier on the ride home. Maybe working with Dillon wouldn't be too bad after all.

2

Meeting the Animals

On Monday morning, after assembly, the students in Mrs. Todd's class got their things together.

Woodbridge Farm Park was just outside the village — close enough for the class to walk.

"All right," said Mrs. Todd. "It's time to get into a double line."

Mandy smiled. Mrs. Todd called their double line a "crocodile," and Mandy thought that was a funny name for children standing or walking in twos.

Mrs. Todd gave out clipboards; they had a pen under every clip. "One for each pair," she told them. "You can take turns bringing them to the farm."

Each pair decided who would take the clipboard that day. Then, chatting excitedly, the class crossed the playground to the school gate.

Pam Stanton's dad was one of the day's helpers. When the class started moving, he walked close to Dillon. Mandy wondered if Mrs. Todd had asked him to keep an eye on Dillon.

Besides making the plastic bag that held his boots and the clipboard knock against Mandy's legs a couple of times, Dillon behaved well. But he scowled when Mr. Stanton told them that he'd already visited Woodbridge Farm Park and had seen guinea pigs there.

"What are guinea pigs doing on a farm? I hope we get a real farm animal to learn about,"

Dillon said, turning to Mandy. "A huge pig or a bull, or a billy goat with big horns. I bet *you'd* be scared stiff!"

"I'm not scared of any animal," said Mandy. "And I don't mind if we get a big one or a small one. All animals are interesting." Mandy was determined not to let Dillon spoil things for her.

Dillon's scowl deepened, and Mandy turned away to look around. They had turned onto the long road that led to the farm entrance. There were fields edged with stone walls on either side.

They reached the farm gate, and Mrs. Todd watched carefully to make sure the last person through closed it properly.

A tall, friendly looking man came up to greet them. "Now then," he said. "Welcome to Woodbridge Farm Park, everyone. I'm Farmer Woodbridge. I'm sure you're all excited to see the animals you'll be learning about and helping to look after for your project. Mr. Marsh, the farm manager, will take you to see them soon. But first you'd better come into the big barn over there and change into your boots."

The barn smelled of apples and hay and of wood from years past. It wasn't used for storing hay or apples anymore but as a refreshment area. The tables and seats were made out of tree trunks. "You will be coming in here for your morning break," said Farmer Woodbridge.

"And for Question Time," said Mrs. Todd. She had already told the class that the last ten minutes of every visit would be for asking questions about the farm.

Everyone changed into their boots quickly, and the farmer led them outside to where Mr. Marsh was waiting for them. Mrs. Todd told them that they would look at all the animals first, and then she'd give them their animal assignments.

"This morning you will see the farm, make friends with your project animal, and write down any questions you'd like answered in today's Question Time," said Farmer Woodbridge.

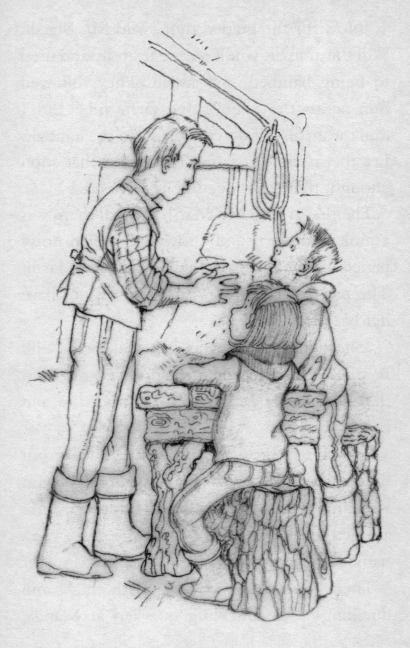

"Now for the guided tour," said Mr. Marsh. "All the animals you'll see are friendly and used to being handled," he added. They followed him across the cobblestone farmyard. "But I don't want any of you to run up to the animals. Let them come to you. They'll do that soon enough; they love meeting new friends."

The first animal Mr. Marsh showed them was a pink, plump, friendly sow with seven noisy piglets. "Her name is Sally," said Mr. Marsh. The pig ambled to the gate of her sty to have her back scratched.

"She doesn't look at all like you, Sally!" Jill Redfern laughed, when they moved off from the pigsty. Sally Martin was tall and thin and had jet-black hair.

The three big white geese hissed a lot, but they made Mandy laugh. Lucy and William Kaye, the twins who were new this term, were amazed to discover that two of the geese were named Lucy and Kay!

There were hens and ducks with chicks and ducklings. One duckling quacked at Mandy, and she felt sure it was Dillon! There were two goats and some brown pigs with black stripes. In a petting corner for smaller children they saw the guinea pigs that Mr. Stanton had mentioned. And Molly, the black-and-white farm dog, had three six-week-old puppies.

Soon they came to Jester, a pretty Jersey cow the color of butterscotch. Mr. Marsh told them that the farm's main herd of cows were Ayrshires. "Jester's what we call a house cow. She's milked by hand, and we use her milk in the refreshment area. She's smaller than an Ayrshire. You'll see that when I show you Clover."

Clover was red and white, and she had horns. "Don't let the horns worry you; Clover's as gentle as a lamb," said Mr. Marsh, with a broad smile. "Which leads us to Snowy."

Snowy was a tiny white lamb. The farm manager told them that her mother had gotten sick, and Snowy had been born early. "Sadly, her mother died," he explained. "So we're rearing little Snowy by hand, which means feeding her milk from a baby's bottle."

Mandy closed her eyes and made a wish. Now that she'd seen Snowy, she knew which animal she wanted to look after most of all!

After meeting all the animals, they went back into the barn for a midmorning snack and to meet more of the people who helped out with visitors. Then, to Mandy's delight, Mrs. Todd chose animals for everyone. She and Dillon were given Snowy the lamb!

"Off you go," said Mrs. Todd when she'd finished calling out names. "And remember to take your clipboards with you."

"I don't believe it!" Dillon muttered crossly. He and Mandy were walking across the farmyard to the field where low wooden fences and a gate made a large pen for Snowy. He put his hands over the top rail of the gate and shook it. "A stupid little lamb!"

Snowy skipped toward them, clambered onto the hay bale near the gate, and stuck her head over the top rail.

"She's gorgeous," said Mandy, rubbing Snowy's head. "And look!" she added, laughing when Snowy rubbed her chin over one of Dillon's hands. "She wants you to pet her, too, Dillon!"

"Well, that's her problem," said Dillon. "I'm not petting a silly lamb!" To Mandy's horror, Dillon snatched his hand away and shoved Snowy. The lamb lost her balance and slipped off the hay bale. And just as Snowy let out a loud bleat, Mandy saw Farmer Woodbridge coming toward them!

3

Snowy

"Now then, Dillon. There's nothing Snowy likes better than a gentle game of push and shove. But right now, she'll be thinking more of her tummy. Her feed's due in about ten minutes."

Farmer Woodbridge turned to Mandy and gave her a reassuring wink. "Mandy, isn't it?"

he asked, and Mandy nodded. "Well, Mandy, how about running across to the farm kitchen and asking Mrs. Woodbridge for Snowy's bottle? It's the building next to the small barn. You can both watch me feed Snowy, and then tomorrow you or Dillon can have a try."

Dillon sniffed loudly and scuffed one foot over a stone that was sunk into the ground. Mandy gave him a worried glance before going off to find Mrs. Woodbridge.

The kitchen door of the farmhouse was open.

"Come in, dear," said the dark-haired lady who was standing by an old-fashioned stove. "I'm Mrs. Woodbridge. I'll be meeting your class later in the big barn. Right now, I'm busy fixing feeds."

Mandy beamed and thought Mrs. Woodbridge looked just the way a farmer's wife should look. She was plump and had dark eyes that twinkled and rosy cheeks. "Farmer Woodbridge sent me to ask you for Snowy's bottle," Mandy said.

"It's all ready for her." Mrs. Woodbridge reached for the feeding bottle. It had Snowy's name on it. "And what do you think of our orphan lamb?" she asked as she handed Mandy the bottle.

"She's perfect!" Mandy replied. "But it's too bad she has no other lambs to play with."

"She will have playmates in a week or two," said Mrs. Woodbridge. "Though I think she'll always like people better than lambs, because it's people who feed her."

"Farmer Woodbridge said we can watch while he feeds her, and tomorrow one of us can feed her," said Mandy.

"Yes, you're working in twos, aren't you? I expect someone will have to toss a coin to decide which of you feeds her first."

"I don't think Dillon will want to!" Mandy said before she could stop herself.

"Really? Maybe he thinks looking after a lamb is easy. Just tell him that lambs aren't as easy to handle as he might think. You have to be tough, strong, and healthy to work with sheep. You'll know what I mean when you see Snowy drinking her milk."

Mandy hurried back across the farmyard. She held Snowy's bottle carefully in one hand. She was still a few yards away from the pen when Snowy started bleating. At first the *baa*s were low and quiet. As Mandy got closer, they became louder and high-pitched. The little lamb began to run backward and forward across the top of the hay bale.

"Yes, Snowy. You're quite right. Your feed's here," said Farmer Woodbridge, laughing at the little creature.

"Did she see the bottle, or could she smell the milk?" Mandy asked, handing it to Farmer Woodbridge.

"A bit of both, I expect," the farmer replied. He checked the nipple to make sure it was firmly on, then he held the bottle toward Snowy. By now, the lamb was stretching her head over the top of the gate.

"You need a strong wrist for this," he said. Snowy took the nipple eagerly. "She may be small, but she's got plenty of strength. When she's as hungry as this, I always stand outside the pen to feed her."

"Do you mean she could pull you over if you were inside with her?" Mandy asked.

"Not pull me over exactly," the farmer replied. "But she could certainly pull the nipple off the bottle and lose all the milk! I like feeding time to be as peaceful as possible. It's better for Snowy then. Ah, that's it," he added. "She's sucking nicely now. It always takes a minute or two before she realizes sucking is better than pulling."

Mandy watched, fascinated, as Snowy began to suck energetically. Then she laughed. Milk dribbled from the corners of the lamb's mouth.

"I don't see what's so funny!" said Dillon sulkily.

Mandy ignored Dillon's remark.

"She tries to drink it too quickly, that's her problem," said Farmer Woodbridge. "And look, when the bottle's emptying, you have to tilt it to make sure Snowy's swallowing milk and not air."

"Why?" asked Dillon.

Mandy's eyes widened in surprise. Dillon was interested enough to ask a question!

"If she swallowed air, she'd get a tummy ache," Farmer Woodbridge replied. "If that were to happen, we might have trouble getting her to drink her milk the next time. Then she'd start to lose weight, and that's something we don't want to happen."

Snowy soon finished the bottle. Farmer Woodbridge gave her a quick pat and turned to look at Mandy and Dillon. "She'll empty her bladder now that she's had her milk. After she's done that, you can go in the pen with her. She won't be so feisty now that she's full."

"Thanks, Farmer Woodbridge," said Mandy.

Farmer Woodbridge smiled. "Just remember to shut the gate behind you," he said. "I'm going to see how everybody else is doing."

As the farmer walked away, Mandy thought about writing down what they had just learned.

She wanted to record Snowy's feeding in their project book when they got back to school. She looked around for their clipboard. Dillon had been holding it when Mrs. Todd had given out the animal assignments. She remembered Dillon twanging the strong clip against the board, but she couldn't remember seeing it after that.

"Dillon, do you know where our clipboard is?" she asked.

Dillon turned to her and scowled. "I dropped it on our way over here," he said. "We don't need it anyway. There's not much you can write down about a lamb."

"But there's lots to write about already, Dillon," Mandy insisted.

"Like what?" Dillon challenged, climbing over the gate to get into Snowy's pen.

"Like the way Snowy jumped up on the hay bale to make friends with us, and the way she bleated when she saw me coming with her bottle, and how quickly she finished the milk, and —"

"You sound like a lamb yourself!" said Dillon, rudely. "Bleat, bleat, bleat."

He hadn't meant to be funny, but Mandy giggled. Snowy skipped up to look curiously at Dillon. "Snowy thought you were bleating at *her*," she said. And, to her amazement, Mandy was almost sure that she saw a flicker of a smile on Dillon's face.

But then he shrugged. "Well, if you think writing things down is so important, *you* go and look for the clipboard," he said, glaring at Mandy.

"Fine," Mandy replied quietly. She reached over to rub Snowy's head. "At least you're nice and friendly, aren't you, Snowy?" she whispered.

Mandy remembered her promise to herself not to be bothered when Dillon wasn't very nice. I just hope it won't bother Snowy, either, she thought.

Mandy found the clipboard easily. Dillon had dropped it just outside the entrance to the barn.

As she approached Snowy's pen, the little lamb began to bleat loudly once again.

"It's not your bottle, you silly lamb," said Dillon.

It was the first time Mandy had heard Dillon actually speak to Snowy, but she didn't want Dillon to realize she'd noticed. She quickly went into the pen, sat down on the hay bale, pulled the pen from under the clip, and started writing on the first sheet of paper.

Dillon climbed over the gate and wandered off.

After a while, he came back into the pen and looked over Mandy's shoulder. "You're doing lots of writing," he said. "But I bet you don't have any good questions to ask."

"You're right," said Mandy in dismay. "I haven't thought of any questions." She looked down at Snowy, who was stretched out on the ground next to the hay bale, sleeping. "We don't know how old she is. We can ask that."

"That's boring," Dillon said. "All this stupid lamb does is eat and sleep. I've just seen Andrew Pearson. One of the ducklings is stranded in the middle of the duck pond. Andrew and Mr. Marsh both have a big net to see if one of them can scoop the duckling up. That's what I call exciting!"

"Well, you can do something for Snowy tomorrow," Mandy told him. "You can try feeding her with her bottle."

"What do you mean, *try*?" Dillon demanded. "You think I won't be able to do it?"

Mandy hadn't meant that at all. Before she had time to say anything, Dillon added, "Well, just you wait, Mandy Hope. I'll teach you *and* that stupid lamb!"

Mrs. Todd called them just then. It was time to gather in the big barn to ask their questions.

Mandy hurried off ahead of Dillon. She'd had enough of him for the day. Besides, she was worried about what Dillon had said. She hoped he wasn't going to bully little Snowy tomorrow!

4

A Few Surprises

Mrs. Todd stood in the doorway of the barn and had a quick look at everyone's clipboard as they went in.

"Now," she said when they were settled. "There won't be time for all of you to have your questions answered today. Besides, you'll find some of the answers for yourselves as the week goes on. For now, think carefully and pick out questions that involve numbers, so that we can talk about them in this afternoon's math lesson."

"How old is Snowy?" Dillon whispered mockingly to Mandy. "The answer to that won't give us much to work out in math, will it?"

"No, it won't," Mandy agreed. "But that's okay. I've just thought of a much better question."

When their turn came, Mandy asked how much milk Snowy had at each feed.

"At the moment she has around three ounces every four hours," answered Mrs. Woodbridge. "She sleeps in the small barn next to the farmhouse, and one of us gets up to give her a bottle during the night."

The others took turns asking their questions, and then it was time to put their shoes on and head back to school. "As quickly as you can, please," said Mrs. Todd. "We're already running a few minutes late."

On their way, Dillon picked up a sturdy branch that was lying on the ground under an oak tree. "Watch this!" he said to Mandy. Then he broke the branch in two. "See how strong I am?" he asked as he threw the pieces down.

Mandy didn't say anything. She guessed that Dillon was trying to scare her, and she wasn't going to let on that, in a way, he had.

The afternoon seemed to go quickly. Math was much more fun than usual. Mandy counted up how many bottles of milk Snowy had in a day and in a week. Then she started to figure out how many pints of milk that added up to. She was surprised when Dillon came up with the answer almost right away.

"It's 3,780 milliliters — that's about a gallon. I was figuring it out on the way back to school," he said when Mandy commented on how quick he'd been. Then he scowled and added, "There wasn't much else to think about, except how boring it was this morning."

Mandy sighed. Every time she thought Dillon was starting to get interested in Snowy, he would say something to make her believe he really wasn't interested at all! She wished Mrs. Todd had paired her with somebody else — or that James was at school. At least she could have told him about Snowy during lunchtime or on their way home.

When Mandy was leaving school there was a surprise for her. She was at the school gate with Jill and Sarah, and James *was* there! He was surrounded by some of his classmates, and he had Blackie with him.

"My mom said it was such a nice day that it would be all right to come to school for half an hour," he told them as Mandy and Sarah crouched down to stroke Blackie. "Anyway, I wanted to hear about your trip to the farm, Mandy. Did you see Dillon the duck?"

"One of the smaller ducks quacked at me," Mandy told him. "I *think* it was Dillon. But there are lots of ducks that same size, and they all look alike."

"They don't when you get to know them," said Andrew Pearson, who joined them. "You'll have to come and have a good look at them tomorrow, Mandy. Then you'll see that they're all different. The one I rescued from the middle of the pond is tamer than the others. I bet that it's Dillon."

"Which animal did Mrs. Todd choose for you?" James asked Mandy.

"A boring, stupid lamb," said Dillon, who'd just walked through the gate with his sister.

Mandy glanced at James. "I'll tell you about it on the way home," she said.

James nodded and then smiled at Samantha, who had stopped to stroke Blackie. "Oh, James! What a beautiful dog!" she said.

Blackie wagged his tail and pushed his way between Jill and Sarah to get close to Samantha. But Dillon hauled her away. "Just leave the dog alone and come on," he said.

"What was all that about?" asked James as Dillon marched off, with Samantha following.

Mandy shook her head. "I don't know, James. I just don't understand Dillon at all."

"I don't know why you even want to try," said Sarah Drummond. "He's nothing but a pain."

"Well, you can't say he was looking after Samantha *then*, James," said Mandy. "It's not like she's scared of dogs. She *wanted* to pet Blackie."

"He was just being a bully, as usual," said Jill Redfern. And Mandy had to agree that was how it had looked.

A few minutes later, as they made their way toward the village green, Mandy told James all about Snowy.

"And Dillon doesn't like her?" said James.

"I'm not sure about that," Mandy replied. "I think maybe he does, but he just won't admit it."

"Maybe he thinks liking any animal would make him seem nice," James suggested. "Maybe that's why he dragged Samantha away from Blackie."

"Perhaps," Mandy said. "But it's worse with Snowy, because she's so tiny and young, and Dillon thinks there isn't much to learn about a lamb. He said all Snowy does is eat and sleep. He was really rough with her. And he threatened to teach me *and* Snowy a lesson tomorrow."

"I wouldn't worry too much, Mandy," said James. "He was probably just talking."

"Maybe," Mandy said doubtfully. "I hope so . . ."

James lived at the other end of Welford. He and Mandy split up by the big oak tree on the green and went their separate ways.

Mrs. Robbins, Welford's community nurse, was just coming out of the clinic when Mandy arrived at Animal Ark.

"Hello, Nurse Robbins," she said. "Hello, Gareth." Mandy held a hand out toward the friendly sandy-colored retriever.

Gareth had once been a guide dog for the blind. When he became too old to work, Mrs. Robbins gave him a home. At first,

Gareth didn't settle down at all. Mrs. Robbins guessed that he missed being a working dog. So she started taking him with her to visit some of her housebound patients. The experiment worked even better than expected. Gareth became happier and livelier, and so did Nurse Robbins's patients. They loved seeing Gareth.

"I've just been making an appointment for his booster shot," Mrs. Robbins told Mandy.

"And are you going to go and cheer someone up now, Gareth?" Mandy asked.

"I'm taking him home before I make my next visit," said Mrs. Robbins. "I'm going to see Mrs. Lewis. She loves dogs, but she's allergic to dog hairs. They make her cough very badly."

"Is Mrs. Lewis related to Dillon Lewis?" Mandy asked.

"She's his grandmother," said Mrs. Robbins. "She lives with his family. Dillon is very good with her."

"He is?" said Mandy. She was surprised.

Mrs. Robbins nodded. "Mrs. Lewis is a big, heavy woman, but little Dillon manages to help her from her bed to her chair. Sometimes she has to drink from a special cup, and Dillon's the only one who can get her to do it. He spends a lot of time with her. I'm afraid his big brothers tease him about that."

Mandy rubbed Gareth's head. She noticed a couple of his hairs on her skirt. "What if you had some of Gareth's hairs on your uniform, Nurse Robbins? Would that make Mrs. Lewis cough?"

"I don't think so, Mandy. But I don't take any chances. I always take a clean white coat with me when I go to see her. Anyway, I thought you wanted to be a vet," she said, "not a doctor."

"I do want to be a vet," said Mandy. "I was just wondering . . ."

Mrs. Robbins's beeper sounded just then, and she had to hurry off to answer her car phone. But the community nurse had given Mandy a lot to think about. Now perhaps she understood why Dillon had dragged his sister away from Blackie. Maybe Dillon was worried in case Samantha got dog hairs on her. Maybe he was just looking out for his grandmother.

Later, while she was having her hot chocolate before bed, Mandy told her parents all about her day. Dr. Emily asked how she and Dillon were getting along.

Mandy made a face. "Not very well, and I was worried that he might bully Snowy if he does feed her tomorrow. But now I'm not so sure." Mandy told her what she had learned about Dillon from the community nurse.

"I bet Dillon's worried that you will tease him, like Nurse Robbins says his brothers do," said Dr. Emily.

"I wouldn't do that!" Mandy said. "But I hope Snowy doesn't do anything to make me laugh while Dillon's feeding her. He might think I'm laughing at him. She was so funny today. She sucked so hard that the milk dribbled out of her mouth."

Dr. Adam Hope chuckled. "Well, you've certainly managed to get your hot chocolate all around the outside of *your* mouth. Time to wash your face and go to bed!"

Mandy smiled back, then said good night to her parents.

"Don't read for too long, Mandy," said Dr. Emily.

"I won't," Mandy promised. "I want to be wide awake tomorrow!"

5

An Awful Mistake

The next morning when Mandy woke up, her bedroom looked dull and gloomy. She jumped out of bed and hurried over to the window to see if it was raining. It wasn't, but it must have been raining all night. There were big puddles on the garden path and droplets of water dripping from the branches of the trees.

The sky was gray when Mandy's class set off. Mandy had been worried that Mrs. Todd might call off today's farm visit. But she told them that Farmer Woodbridge had special buildings for the animals when the weather was bad.

The sun came out by the time they reached the farm, but the ground was wet and muddy. It was a good thing Mrs. Todd had told her class to wear their boots for the walk to and from the farm today; there were puddles all over the farmyard.

Farmer Woodbridge came out of one of the barns to greet them. "Apart from the ducks," he said, laughing as a crowd of ducks waddled past, quacking and paddling in the puddles, "we've put the animals you're working with in their barns or shippons."

"A shippon is a cowshed," Carrie Anderson said. "One of the farm helpers told me yesterday when she was watching Gary and me with Clover."

"So you've learned something new already

today," Mrs. Todd told the others. "Now take your backpacks into the big barn. After that you can find your animals. And remember, as friendly as the animals may be, any gates or barriers are there for your protection as well as theirs. No going inside without permission."

As they hurried over to the big barn, Mandy pointed out that some of the buildings around the farmyard had an animal's name on a little board screwed to the door.

"I noticed that ages ago," said Dillon. "Snowy's in that small barn next to the farm-house."

"Oh, yes," Mandy remembered. "Mrs. Wood-bridge told us Snowy slept in there. I can't wait to see her again," she added. She put her back-pack on one of the log benches and opened it to get the clipboard out in case they wanted to make any notes. It was her turn to bring it to-day. "Come on, Dillon," she said. "Let's hurry."

When Mandy and Dillon were making their way to Snowy's barn, one of the young ducks waddled up to Mandy. She felt sure it was Dillon. She crouched down to stroke the duckling.

"That's the same one I scooped out of the pond yesterday," said Andrew Pearson. "I told you she was much tamer than the others."

Mandy saw Mrs. Todd looking at her and decided she'd better hurry off to join Dillon.

She heard Snowy's high-pitched bleats from a distance. When she went into the barn, she saw that Snowy had a large pen behind metal gates that ran right across the width of the barn. Dillon was in the pen with Snowy.

"Dillon!" Mandy exclaimed. "We're not supposed to go through gates without permission! You'll get us all into trouble if Mrs. Todd sees you in there."

Mandy reached the gates and stared in horror. Dillon had hold of Snowy's tail! The little lamb was struggling to get away from him.

"What are you doing? Stop pulling her tail!" she cried.

"I wasn't pulling her tail," Dillon snapped as Snowy struggled away from him. "There's something wound tightly around it. I'm trying to get whatever it is off. But the silly lamb won't keep still. Don't just stand there, Mandy! Come and help me."

Mandy threw the clipboard down and climbed over the gate. Snowy, still bleating noisily, ran to her and jumped up, just like a puppy. Her tail wagged fast from side to side, but when Mandy leaned forward she could see what Dillon was talking about. Something that looked like a thick rubber band was wound round Snowy's tail, about four and a half inches from the end.

Mandy felt terrible. She'd made an awful mistake in thinking that Dillon had been tormenting Snowy. She started to tell Dillon she was sorry.

"I don't care what you thought, Mandy. Just think how we can get this off Snowy's tail. It must be hurting her!"

"Now then, you two. What are you doing

inside the pen? Is something wrong?" At the sound of Farmer Woodbridge's voice, Snowy leaped away from Mandy and ran to the metal gate.

"We're trying to help Snowy," said Dillon. "There's something on her tail."

Farmer Woodbridge came closer but didn't say a word. His lips were clamped in a tight, straight line. Thinking he was angry, Mandy said anxiously, "We didn't do it! Really we didn't."

"It's all right, I know that, Mandy. There's nothing to worry about." Farmer Woodbridge didn't sound angry. In fact it sounded as if he might laugh.

He climbed over the gate and lifted Snowy into his arms. He walked over to sit on a hay bale, spread the lamb across his knees, and told Mandy and Dillon to come closer.

He put his hand under Snowy's tail so that it lay across his palm. "*I* put this rubber ring around Snowy's tail a month ago, when she was just a day or so old," he said. "It was there yesterday, you just didn't notice it!"

He smiled as Snowy wriggled closer to him and stuck her head inside his jacket. "She'll have a little snooze now," he said.

"But why did you do it?" asked Dillon urgently.

The farmer explained how the rubber band gradually stops the blood supply from reaching the end of Snowy's tail. "Eventually, that bit of it withers away and then falls off. It's —"

"It's terrible!" Dillon interrupted, his face getting red. "*Why* do you want to make the end of her tail fall off?"

"It's what we call docking," the farmer said. "You see, as lambs grow, their wool grows, too. It gets longer and thicker. If we left all of little Snowy's tail on, she'd have lots of thick wool for muck to cling to. Flies like muck; they like to lay eggs on it. The eggs hatch into maggots, and the maggots would start to nibble at Snowy's skin."

"Oh! That sounds horrible!" Mandy shuddered.

Farmer Woodbridge nodded. "It can happen anywhere on a sheep, so we always keep a careful watch. We use special sprays, and a couple of times a year we bathe the sheep in something that helps to keep the flies away. But the fewer places for the flies to go in the first place, the better," he said.

"Poor Snowy," Mandy sighed, looking at the lamb's tail again. "Having this tight rubber band around her tail can't feel good."

"It probably feels a little strange at times," Farmer Woodbridge agreed. "But I'm sure it doesn't hurt her," he said, looking at Dillon. "There are lots of things that don't seem nice, but we have to do them to keep the animals healthy."

"Like shots," Mandy offered. "People and animals have them. They're not very nice, but they help stop you from getting sick, don't they?"

"And medicine," said Dillon. "Some medicines taste awful, but they make you better."

It was the first time Dillon had spoken for a while, and Mandy turned to smile at him. He even sounded friendly and interested.

Dillon didn't smile back, though, and Mandy turned away from his hard gaze. "I'm going to make some notes about Snowy's tail," she said, going to the metal gates. She picked up the clipboard.

Mandy wrote a little, then looked up to ask Dillon if he wanted to write anything down. As he talked with Farmer Woodbridge, Dillon was stroking Snowy. Mandy quickly lowered her head again. She had a feeling Dillon wouldn't want her to see him doing that.

A few minutes later Mrs. Todd stuck her head in the barn door and told Mandy and Dillon it was time for their midmorning break.

Farmer Woodbridge put Snowy down in a bed of hay and said he'd have a break, too. "I'll see you back in here later," he told Dillon and

Mandy. "I bet Snowy will be awake and hungry by then."

It was noisy in the farmyard as everyone arrived and started telling one another what they'd been doing. Mandy was eager to tell Dillon she was sorry for thinking he'd been trying to hurt Snowy. But Dillon walked off toward the boys' bathroom, and Carrie and Sally called Mandy over to sit with them, so she didn't get a chance.

Everyone wanted to get back to their animals, but Mrs. Todd made them wait until fifteen minutes had passed. "The farmworkers want a break, even if you don't," she said with a smile.

"William and I are going to groom the goats after our break," said Sally. "What are you and Dillon going to do, Mandy?"

"Feed Snowy, I hope," said Mandy. She had to apologize to Dillon first, she thought. She glanced across at him, but he walked away.

6

Wrong Again!

Snowy was awake when Mandy and Dillon went back into the smaller barn. She bleated when they entered, and Mandy laughed as the lamb started skipping, hopping, and jumping around the pen.

"It will be nice when more lambs are born

and Snowy has some friends to play with," she said. "It's too bad that she's alone all the time."

She turned to look at Dillon. Maybe now would be a good time to tell him she was sorry about what she'd said earlier. "Dillon, I'm really —"

Dillon interrupted. "Well, you're wrong about Snowy. So there!" he said.

Mandy thought he'd guessed what she wanted to say and wasn't going to let her finish. She decided not to say any more about it. She'd just try to be friendly. "What do you mean, I'm wrong?" she asked.

"The animals are only on their own while we're here," Dillon continued. "William Kaye said Mr. Marsh told him that when we've gone, the goats, Snowy, and the hens are all let into the paddock together."

"That's good." Mandy smiled. "Oh, that reminds me, Sally made a drawing of one of the goats. She showed it to me during break. We haven't made any sketches of Snowy yet. She's standing still now, nibbling at some hay. Do you want to do a drawing, Dillon?"

Dillon shook his head.

"All right," said Mandy. "I'll do one." She took a sheet of drawing paper from the clipboard and placed the clipboard on the metal gates. "Just keep still for a while longer, Snowy," she whispered. "It'll be much easier to draw you if you aren't jumping around all over the place."

But Snowy only stayed still for a few more seconds. Then she skipped over to a small plastic barrel attached to the back of the pen. When Snowy started to nibble the bottom of the barrel, Mandy gasped. What if Snowy swallowed some of the plastic and got a tummy ache?

She threw her clipboard down, climbed over the gate, and moved quickly toward the lamb. "Dillon," she called as she went, "go get help! I think Snowy might have swallowed some plastic!"

To Mandy's relief, Dillon did as she asked, looking worried himself.

When Mandy got nearer to the barrel, she bent down and stretched her arms out in front of her. She slowly stepped closer to Snowy. Just as Mandy was about to lift Snowy away, she saw four short plastic tubes sticking out around the bottom of the barrel. Snowy wasn't chewing, she was sucking at one of them. Around Snowy's mouth, Mandy could now see milk.

Mandy heard heavy footsteps and turned to see Farmer Woodbridge. He was leaning on the metal gate next to Dillon, and he had a broad smile on his face.

Dillon wasn't smiling. He still looked worried.

"I thought Snowy was chewing something she shouldn't," Mandy said, looking at the farmer. "But now I can see that this is here for her to suck, right?"

Farmer Woodbridge nodded. "Come," he said to Dillon. "Jump over and I'll show you and Mandy how this works."

Farmer Woodbridge told them that the barrel was called a lamb adopter. "The idea is that lambs who aren't being fed by their moms can get a drink of milk from the lamb adopter whenever they feel like it," he explained.

Mandy had often seen lambs skip up to their moms, have a little drink, and skip away again. The lamb adopter provided almost the same thing.

"We use warm milk for Snowy's bottle, but the milk mixture we put inside the barrel is made with cold water," the farmer said, lifting the lid so Mandy and Dillon could see inside. "When Snowy sucks at one of the tubes, the milk comes through.

"The lamb adopter is like a human baby's cup," he continued. "Except here, there's room for four lambs to drink at the same time."

"It's not just babies who have special cups," said Dillon. "Sometimes grown-ups have to use them, too."

"That's right," the farmer agreed. "Good point."

Mandy guessed that Dillon was thinking of his grandma. She waited to see if he would say anything else, but he didn't. He looked away, embarrassed by the farmer's praise, and began kicking his boot against the wall.

Snowy lifted her head and started to move away from the lamb adopter.

"Dillon! You've disturbed Snowy!" Mandy said.

The lamb bleated, went over to Farmer Woodbridge, and banged her head against his knees.

"That has nothing to do with Dillon," said the farmer. "Snowy's letting me know she wants her bottle. She doesn't really like sucking her milk from a tube. She always gives up after a minute or two. That's why we have to bottle-feed her."

"Should I get her bottle?" Mandy asked. She laughed as Snowy started banging into her legs, too. "Snowy's saying, 'Yes, please,'" she joked. She crouched down to stroke the lamb and laughed again as Snowy tried to climb onto her lap.

"You two stay here and play with her while I get her bottle," said the farmer. "And you know what they say about worry turning people's hair gray. Try not to find anything else to worry about while I'm gone, or you'll both be going back to school with hair as white as Snowy's!"

Dillon leaned back against the hay bale and watched Snowy jumping on and off Mandy's lap. "My mom's got lots of gray hairs," he said suddenly. "I bet that's because she worries a lot about my grandma."

"Does your grandma live with you?" Mandy asked. She knew the answer, of course, but she was trying to get Dillon to talk.

"What if she does?" Dillon said. "You're always asking questions, Mandy. And when you're not asking questions, you're busy telling people off for things you *think* they're doing."

"Look, I know I made a mistake, but I *tried*

to tell you I was sorry for thinking that you were pulling Snowy's tail!" Mandy protested.

Snowy *baa*ed and Mandy stroked her. Then the little lamb did something that made Mandy forget all about apologizing to Dillon. "Oh, Dillon, look!" she said. "Snowy's trying to suck my fingers!" Snowy sucked so hard that Mandy couldn't pull her fingers away. "You are a funny little thing, Snowy," Mandy said, laughing.

Mandy turned to Dillon. "She should go back to the lamb adopter if she's so hungry, shouldn't she?"

"Are you getting mad at me, Mandy?" Dillon replied, sounding angry. "You were wrong *again*, you know, when you said I had made Snowy stop drinking from it!"

"I *wasn't* mad at you!" said Mandy. "I was —"

"Oh, shut up, Mandy," Dillon interrupted. He pushed his way past her and Snowy, leaped over the metal gate, and dashed out of the barn.

Mandy heard a muffled exclamation from

outside. After a short silence she heard Farmer Woodbridge's deep voice, but she couldn't hear what he was saying. But she certainly heard Dillon when he shouted, "I don't want to feed Snowy. Let Mandy do it. Snowy likes her, and Mandy likes Snowy."

Mandy felt awful. She never seemed to find the right thing to say to Dillon, even when she was trying to apologize to him. She was willing to be his friend, but Dillon only wanted to see things *his* way.

After another minute or so Farmer Woodbridge came in with Snowy's bottle.

Snowy dashed to the metal gate, bleating excitedly. Mandy followed, her eyes on the barn door. She was wondering if Dillon would come back in and what she could say to him if he did.

"Mr. Marsh took Dillon to show him around our museum," the farmer told her, climbing into the pen. "There's lots of old farm equipment in there," he added. "Things that my great-great-grandfather used when he farmed sheep here. You can go if you like," he added. "But I thought you'd rather feed Snowy."

"Oh, I'd love to feed her," Mandy replied. "Should I get out of the pen?"

"I think we can chance staying inside with her," said the farmer. "The little drink she had earlier has made her a little less hungry. You can hook your arm through the bar of the gate if Snowy pulls too hard!"

He brought his hand from behind his back and handed Mandy the bottle. "Squeeze the nipple so that the milk comes into it," he said. "That might encourage her to suck instead of pull. Be as quick as you can, Mandy. I'll try to hold her still while you're doing it, or she'll jump up and knock you over!"

Snowy was bleating louder and louder and struggling to get away from Farmer Wood-bridge. Mandy squeezed the nipple, and when a drop of milk appeared through the hole, she held the bottle toward the lamb. Snowy grabbed the nipple and started sucking noisily.

"Gosh!" Mandy gasped. "You *do* need a strong wrist to keep hold of the bottle!"

Farmer Woodbridge nodded and watched, ready to help Mandy. Snowy was pulling hard, and Mandy almost lost hold of the bottle a couple of times. But she soon got the hang of things, and she watched proudly as Snowy sucked and gulped.

"Remember what I told you yesterday about being careful that Snowy doesn't swallow air," the farmer said. "You'll need to tilt the bottle soon."

"Okay," Mandy replied, her eyes glued to the bottle so she could see when it needed tilting.

"That's it. You're doing fine," praised the farmer. His voice was warm and kind. Snowy looked so happy with her eyes half-closed and her tail wagging, Mandy began to feel better.

When Snowy finished her bottle, she wandered away. It wasn't long before the little lamb lay down in the hay and fell asleep, just as she had the previous day.

"Maybe I should go and find Dillon now," said Mandy. "Mrs. Todd might wonder why we've split up."

"Worrying again," said the farmer. "You just stay here. Mrs. Todd knows where Dillon is. In fact," he added with a twinkle in his eye, "she told him he'd have to tell the whole class about the farm's museum in your next history lesson."

"All right," said Mandy, glancing over at Snowy, "I won't worry about Dillon. I'll try to do another drawing of Snowy while she's asleep."

Mandy had finished her picture of Snowy when Mrs. Todd came to tell her it was Question Time.

Dillon came into the barn just as Mandy was showing Sally her picture of Snowy. "It isn't as good as your drawing of the goat," Mandy said.

"It isn't good at all!" said Dillon, peering over Mandy's shoulder. "It looks like something by a five-year-old."

"Well, you do a better one, then!" said Mandy.

"What? So you can laugh at me for drawing?" said Dillon.

"Why would I do that?" said Mandy.

Dillon shrugged and looked away.

Before Mandy could say anything else, Mrs. Todd clapped her hands. Question Time was about to start. But Mandy was determined to try and find out what Dillon had meant.

On the way back to school, Mrs. Todd came to walk next to Mandy and Dillon, and she asked if they'd enjoyed themselves.

Dillon just muttered, "It was okay, I suppose." Mandy smiled and nodded enthusiastically. She told her teacher all about docking lambs' tails and lamb adopters.

"I think the best part was when I fed Snowy her bottle," said Mandy. "Snowy tugged and pulled a lot. My wrist was aching by the time she finished all her milk. But it was really neat!"

"Well, it sounds as if you learned a lot and enjoyed yourself, too," said Mrs. Todd before moving back to talk to some of the others.

Mandy glanced at Dillon. He was scowling. Maybe he felt left out, Mandy thought. But he could have joined in.

"I bet you were glad when I went to see the museum, weren't you?" Dillon said. "It meant you could have Snowy all to yourself and do everything for her!"

"That's not fair, Dillon!" said Mandy. "You could have fed Snowy if you'd stayed."

"I didn't want to, so there," Dillon replied.

Mandy shook her head and sighed. No matter what she said to Dillon, it was the wrong thing.

7

A Step Forward

Mandy was late leaving school at the end of the day. She stayed behind with Terry and Jerry, the class's gerbils, to clean out their cage.

The playground was deserted, but as Mandy got close to the school gate she heard mocking laughter. Then she heard someone say, "So,

Farmer Dillon, did you have a good time to-day? *Baa, baa, baa!*"

Mandy was just in time to see two bigger boys cycling away from Dillon and Samantha. She heard Dillon say furiously to his sister, "That was *your* fault, Samantha, for talking about my farm trip at breakfast this morning! Gary must have told Martin about it!"

"And what are *you* doing here?" he added, as Mandy joined them.

Mandy ignored Dillon and looked at Samantha. "Are they your brothers?" she asked.

"One of them is Gary, our oldest brother," Samantha replied. "The bigger boy is his friend, Martin."

"Just mind your own business, Mandy Hope!" said Dillon. "And you hurry up," he said, tugging Samantha's arm. "You know we told Mom we'd get home as fast as we could."

As Mandy hurried home, she couldn't help feeling sorry for Dillon. It must be awful to have a big brother like Gary.

When Mandy arrived at Animal Ark, Dr. Emily told her that James had called. "He said not to come over, because they've got visitors," she said. Mandy was really disappointed. She really wanted to see James.

"But there's an animal friend of yours in the clinic," Dr. Emily added. "Go get changed, and you can visit him."

Mandy dashed upstairs and quickly changed out of her school clothes. She couldn't wait to see whom her mother was talking about.

"I'm here, Mom," she called as she hurried back downstairs, her feet thumping loudly on each stair.

"I'd never have guessed!" Dr. Emily laughed as Mandy arrived breathlessly at the bottom.

They went through the door that led to the clinic.

"There," said Dr. Emily, holding open the door and pointing to a cage.

"It's Clown!" said Mandy, running forward. "Why's he here, Mom? What's he been up to this time?"

Clown was one of six kittens Mandy and James had found a home for at Westmoor House, a retirement home about a mile out of the village. Before the kittens had gone to their new home, Mandy had looked after them at Animal Ark for a few days. She discovered that Clown was the most mischievous kitten of all.

Dr. Emily opened the cage door and lifted out the black-and-orange kitten. "He pulled a rose out of a vase of flowers," she said. "Before anyone could get to him, he chewed the stem and managed to get a thorn stuck in his gum!"

"Did you get it out?" asked Mandy, taking the kitten from her mom.

"I did, but he put up quite a fight," Dr. Emily replied. "I had to give him something to make him sleepy before I could look in his mouth."

"Oh, Clown!" said Mandy, gently stroking his chest. "You're such a naughty boy!" She glanced up at her mom. "How long will he have to stay?"

"He's well enough to go home now," said Dr. Emily. "I've got a call to make near Westmoor House, so I told Della I'd take Clown back at the same time. I thought you might like to come with me and see Clown's brothers and sisters."

"I sure would!" Mandy laughed.

Dr. Emily nodded. "I'll drop you off and pick you up when I've finished my other call," Dr. Emily said. "We'll have to put Clown in his cat carrier. I'm not so sure he'll like that," she added. "Della said he meowed all the way here when she brought him."

Clown meowed all the way back to Westmoor House, too. Mandy was glad when they got there. She jumped out of the car and rang the front doorbell. Dr. Emily lifted the carrier out.

"Clown's fine," Dr. Emily said when Della Skilton, the home's manager, opened the door.

"He certainly sounds it," Della laughed. She took the carrier from Dr. Emily. "Are you coming in?"

"I have another call, but Mandy would like to visit. Is that all right?" Dr. Emily asked.

"Of course it is," Della replied. "The residents always enjoy seeing her, and Tom will be glad to know Clown's all right. He's done nothing but grumble all afternoon." The residents all shared the kittens, but Tom and Clown were special friends.

Mandy went inside and took Clown out of his carrier. "No, you're not getting down," she told him as he wriggled and struggled. "You're going straight to Tom so you can sit on his lap for a while."

"You aren't the only visitor this afternoon," Della told Mandy as they walked down the long, carpeted corridor to the dayroom. "A new resident arrived this morning. She'll only be staying with us for a week or two, but her grandson's come to see if she's settled in all right."

"Everyone sounds like they're having a good time," said Mandy, hearing loud laughter. No one even seemed to notice Della and Mandy walking into the room. Most of the residents were sitting near the far end of the room with their backs facing the door. They were gathered in a semicircle around someone Mandy couldn't see.

Tom's chair was near one end, and he was the first to see them. "Is that my Clown you've got there?" he said loudly. "Don't know what took you so long. Bring him over here."

"Why don't you take Clown over?" Della told Mandy. "I've got some paperwork to do in the office."

By now, everybody was shuffling and moving. One elderly woman maneuvered her wheelchair to make room for Mandy to reach Tom. Mandy walked through the gap and stopped dead.

"Dillon!"

"Mandy!"

With looks of surprise on both their faces, Mandy and Dillon stared at each other.

"Are you two friends?" said an elderly man called George. "Dillon has come to see his grandma." George pointed to a large, gray-haired woman in a wheelchair. "That's her. She came this morning. Her name is Ethel Lewis. I'm letting her stroke George for a while."

Mandy smiled. It had been her idea to name the kitten after George, who said he didn't like cats. Now the kitten was his special friend.

"Never mind your George, George," grumbled Tom. "Just you hurry up and bring my Clown to me, young Amanda."

Mandy hurried over to put Clown on Tom's lap, and the elderly man smiled. She tried to look cheerful, but finding Dillon here had made her feel a bit uneasy.

"Dillon's been telling us about a lamb he's looking after," said Tom.

"And you've interrupted what he was telling us," said his grandma. "Still, since you have, come over here, and let me get a look at you. What's your name? Amanda?"

"That's my proper name, but almost everyone calls me Mandy, Mrs. Lewis," said Mandy, going to stand in front of the wheelchair.

"Kneel down next to Dillon," Mrs. Lewis said, reaching for her walking stick and pointing to the floor. "It's too much effort for me to look up at you."

Mandy knelt down and started to stroke George. He was orange and black like Clown. "Where are the other kittens?" she asked.

"Well, tell her, Dillon. *You* put them there," said Mrs. Lewis.

"They're all curled up together, sleeping on that blanket on the window seat," Dillon mumbled.

"Now," Mrs. Lewis banged her stick on the floor, "never mind them. They're tired. I want to hear the rest of your story, Dillon."

"Yes, go on!" agreed some of the others.

"Well, what are you waiting for?" Mrs. Lewis demanded. "You were at the part where the silly girl you were with thought the little lamb was eating the bottom of a bucket!"

Mandy gasped and clapped her hand to her mouth.

"I . . . er . . ." Dillon threw a sideways look at Mandy.

"Go on, Dillon," Mandy whispered. "I don't mind. It was pretty silly," she added with a giggle.

Mandy was amazed at the difference in Dillon as he carried on with the story.

He told the residents how worried he was when he ran to get Farmer Woodbridge. "My heart was thumping," he said, "and even though I was running, I felt as if I was moving really slowly."

"Like when you're dreaming that you're trying to get away from somebody," said Tom, "and your legs feel as if they're filled with lead."

Mandy waited for Dillon's scowl to appear, the way it usually did when anybody interrupted him.

But Dillon nodded and smiled. "Yeah. That's

right, Tom!" he said. "It was awful. But when I found Farmer Woodbridge, it was even worse. He didn't seem to mind at all when I told him what little Snowy was doing! And when the two of us got to the barn, he just leaned on the gate and smiled when he saw . . ." Dillon stopped and glanced at Mandy.

"Saw what, Dillon?" his grandma asked.

"The girl's face," said Dillon. "She suddenly realized that Snowy wasn't eating plastic. She was sucking milk from a special feeder."

There was another interruption when the four kittens on the blanket woke up, stretched, and started to play. Dillon helped Mandy pick them up and take them to some of the residents. And he didn't scowl once!

"Well, what did you think of that, Mandy?" asked Mrs. Lewis when Dillon eventually finished the story.

"I think it was really funny," Mandy laughed. "And now I want to tell you something. I was with Dillon when it happened," she said. "And

I was the silly person who thought Snowy was eating the bucket!"

The residents clapped and cheered and laughed some more.

Then George said, "I'm not sure I understand about this special feeder. I don't see *how* a lamb can suck from a bucket."

"I'll draw you a picture of it," Dillon offered.

"There's paper and pencils on that table by the window," George said. "How about drawing a picture of the little lamb as well?"

"Okay!" said Dillon, smiling. He walked over and sat down at the table. Before long, he was hard at work.

"Dillon loves drawing," his grandma said quietly to Mandy. "He's good, too. But he doesn't get a chance to do it at home. His brothers tease him. They think drawing is a baby thing to do."

"Gary was outside school today," said Mandy. "He was with another boy, and they were both teasing Dillon."

Ethel Lewis sniffed. "That must have been Martin. Gary sees a lot of him. They don't have jobs, and they get bored with nothing to do."

Dillon jumped up and took his drawing over to George.

"Ah, now I understand!" chuckled George as he looked carefully at Dillon's picture.

Mandy went over to look at it. Dillon had drawn Snowy sucking at one of the plastic tubes on the lamb adopter. "Dillon! It's great!" she said. "Snowy looks so real! You've even made her tail look as if it's wagging!"

"I told you he was good," his grandma called.

"He's better than good!" Mandy looked down at the drawing again. "I wish you would draw some pictures of Snowy for our project book, Dillon," she said.

"You two can talk about that some other time," Tom grumbled. "Right now, the rest of us are waiting to see Dillon's drawing."

Della came in then and called to Mandy. "Your mom's here to pick you up," she said.

Mandy gave Dillon his drawing and said good-bye. "I'll come to see you all again soon," she said. "And I'll see you tomorrow, Dillon."

"See you, Mandy," Dillon replied. "It's my turn to feed Snowy tomorrow, and maybe I will do some drawings for our project book!"

8

Problems for Mandy

The first thing Mandy saw when she walked into the school playground the next morning was Dillon grabbing a ball from Jill Redfern and running off with it.

"Jill knocked Dillon's sister with her elbow when she was jumping to throw the ball," Pam Stanton told Mandy.

"I didn't mean it," Jill said. "It was an accident. But Dillon's ruined our game now. He's impossible! I don't know how you put up with him at the farm, Mandy."

"It's not so easy," Mandy admitted. "But I was hoping things might be different today."

"Dream on, Mandy!" said Jill. "Dillon will never change."

Just then, Dillon rushed toward them. "Hi, Mandy!" he called. "Do you want to visit my grandma again after school? She said you could. You should have seen what Clown did yesterday, after you left."

"Oh! You've made friends with the school bully?" asked Pam. She gave Mandy an annoyed look. Dillon came to a stop in front of them and stood there bouncing and catching Jill's ball.

Mandy didn't know what to say. Dillon had been so much nicer yesterday at Westmoor House that she didn't want to ignore him now. But she didn't want Jill and Pam to think she was taking Dillon's side.

"Give Jill back her ball, and *then* tell me about Clown," Mandy said. She added, "You really should say you're sorry for ruining their game."

"Yes, you should," said Samantha. "Jill didn't mean to hit me. It was an accident."

Dillon glared at Jill and held the ball toward her. "I'm sorry, okay?"

"It's all right," said Jill. She linked arms with Pam, and they turned and started to walk off. "Coming, Mandy?" she asked over her shoulder.

Mandy rubbed her right foot against her left ankle. She didn't know what to do! "I'll catch up in a minute," she called after them. "I want to hear about Clown first."

By the time Dillon had finished telling Mandy how Clown had climbed up the curtains, and how he used a stepladder to get the kitten down, the bell rang.

They weren't allowed to talk in line, but Pam and Jill both glared at Mandy, and neither of

them spoke to her when they got into the classroom.

Mandy was quiet and thoughtful when Mrs. Todd's class set off for their final walk to the farm. She wanted to show Dillon she was willing to be friends, but did not want Pam and Jill to get upset.

Dillon glanced at her once or twice. Then he said, "Della told me it was you and James Hunter who persuaded her to let the residents have the kittens."

Mandy nodded. "We really wanted the whole litter to have a good home and stay together," she said. "James loves animals as much as I do."

"I like animals, too," Dillon said quietly. "But my brothers think they're for wimps."

"Is that why you pretended not to like Snowy?" Mandy asked. "In case anyone at school made fun of you for liking her?"

"I guess so," Dillon admitted.

"Well, your brothers are wrong," said Mandy. "Farmer Woodbridge isn't a wimp, and he cares about Snowy. And," she continued, "you don't like the way your brothers treat you, but the way you treat everyone at school is even worse!"

Mandy expected Dillon to do or say something really mean after that, but he just stared straight ahead with a sad look on his face.

"Mandy and Dillon! Will you keep up with the rest of us, please!" Mrs. Todd called.

When they caught up with the others, Peter Foster was talking about Timmy, his cairn terrier. "He keeps digging holes under the fence so he can get into the garden next door," he said. "And our neighbor is allergic to dogs. If she gets anywhere near one, she gets all itchy. She has to call us, then one of us has to run out and get him!"

"My grandma's allergic to dogs," said Dillon quietly. "She lives with us, and if any of us bring dog hairs into the house on our clothes, it makes her really sick."

Looking at the others who were listening, Mandy said, "Is that why you wouldn't let

Samantha pet Blackie the other day — in case she got dog hairs on her clothes?"

Dillon looked at the ground and nodded.

Jill Redfern, who was walking in front of Peter and Sarah, turned around. "You should have said so, Dillon," she said. "We all thought you were just bullying Samantha."

"Well, I wasn't!" said Dillon. "And if James is there with Blackie after school today, Samantha can pet Blackie all she wants, because Grandma's spending a few days in Westmoor House."

And, then, to Mandy's relief, Jill smiled at her. They were still friends.

There was no one around when the class reached the farm, so they went straight to the big barn to change into their boots. Soon Mr. Marsh came in. "Things are a bit hectic this morning," he said. "Two of the staff are out sick, and Farmer Woodbridge is busy building nursery pens."

"Nursery pens?" Mandy said. "What are they?"

"They're pens we build on the lower fields at lambing time," said the farm manager. "Each pen has two sections," he explained. "One section is for sheep who are waiting to have their lambs, and the other section is for sheep and newborn lambs."

"That means Snowy will have some lamb friends to play with soon," said Mandy. "That's good."

Mr. Marsh smiled. "At the moment, though, Snowy's in the small barn," he said. "It's a fine day today, so she should be in her outdoor pen. Would you and Dillon like to take her there?"

Mandy glanced at Mrs. Todd, who nodded.

"Yes, please!" Mandy answered.

"She knows you both now," Mr. Marsh said. "She should follow you without any trouble. But just to make sure," he added with a smile, "I'll give you a few lamb pellets each. Let Snowy see you've got them, and she'll certainly follow you. They're her favorite snack."

"One of you take the clipboard," Mrs. Todd

reminded them. "You don't want to have to come back for it."

"It sounds like fun," said Gary Roberts. "Can the rest of us watch them, Mrs. Todd?"

"I don't see why not," Mrs. Todd replied. "As long as you keep quiet. No calling to Snowy or shouting out suggestions to Mandy and Dillon," she added.

Mandy smothered a groan. She wondered if Dillon would be all right with the rest of the class watching them take care of little Snowy. She felt nervous as the two of them went over to Snowy's barn with Mr. Marsh.

9

Nothing But a Bully!

Snowy greeted them noisily. Mr. Marsh pointed to a metal bin and told Mandy and Dillon to open it and take a few pellets. "Make sure you put the lid back on firmly," he said. "We don't want rats and mice getting into the food."

"Is that why you use a metal bin?" Dillon asked. "So they can't nibble holes in it?"

"That's right," said Mr. Marsh, laughing as Snowy bleated louder and pushed hard against the metal gate. "She's seen what you've got. You can both start walking. I'll open the gate for her."

When Mandy and Dillon had only taken a few steps across the farmyard, Snowy caught up with them. She pranced and danced at Dillon's side and banged her head against his clenched hand.

"Stop it, you silly lamb," Dillon said, laughing.

Snowy suddenly stood still, her head raised. She looked up at Dillon. Then she gave a long, drawn-out bleat.

"Okay," said Dillon. "You win. You can have one pellet . . ." He held one out. "Hey! Did you see that?" he asked Mandy. "She nearly ate my fingers, too!"

A ripple of laughter came from their classmates over by the barn.

Mandy sighed with relief when she saw that Dillon was still smiling.

"All right, Snowy," he said, stooping to lift the little lamb, turning her around until she was facing in the right direction. "Let's go. No more pellets until we get there."

This time Snowy skipped along behind Dillon without trying to get at the pellets.

When they reached the pen, Dillon turned to Mandy and said, "Leave this to me. I'll get her safely in."

He opened the gate and then got behind Snowy. "In you go," he said, giving her a gentle push. He closed the gate behind her. He leaned over the gate and stretched his palm toward her so she could eat the rest of the pellets.

"That's going to be a great picture," called Mrs. Todd, who had her camera.

"Well done, Dillon!" called Farmer Woodbridge, hurrying toward them from the far end of the field.

"You've got the makings of a sheep farmer in you," he added when he got close.

Dillon turned red with embarrassment.

"You could be an artist, too," said Mandy. "That drawing you did at Westmoor House yesterday was really good, Dillon. Are you going to do some drawings for our project book?"

"I wouldn't mind making a sketch of you, Farmer Woodbridge," Dillon said, glancing at him. "I know you're busy, but it wouldn't take long," he added.

"All right, I think that I can spare a few minutes," the farmer said.

Mandy smiled and handed Dillon the clipboard. "I'll talk to Snowy while you're drawing," she said.

Farmer Woodbridge was very impressed when Dillon showed him the sketch. "Mandy's right!" he said. "You could be an artist. That's real talent. But now I must get some work done. Would one of you like to fill a bucket of water from the farmyard tap to fill Snowy's trough?"

"I'll do it," Mandy offered. "Dillon can do some more sketches."

The ducks were waddling around by the tap. Mandy stopped to talk to them for a while. Then one of Molly's puppies ran toward her, followed by Lucy Kaye.

"Try to catch him, Mandy!" Lucy yelled. "He wriggled out of my hands when I was putting him in his playpen."

Mandy managed to catch the puppy. She carried him, wriggling and squirming, over to Lucy.

"Good job!" said Pam Stanton, who was standing next to Lucy with one of the other puppies in her arms.

After petting both puppies, Mandy hurried back to fill the bucket.

When Mrs. Todd walked past and told Mandy it was time for morning break, Mandy realized that she'd spent a long time with ducks and puppies!

"I'll have to fill Snowy's trough and come right back, Mrs. Todd," said Mandy.

Dillon helped Mandy empty the water into

the trough, because Snowy kept jumping up to see what was in the bucket.

"We'd better hurry," Mandy said. They carefully closed the pen's gate behind them. "We're missing break time in the barn."

After break, Mrs. Todd decided to take a picture of the class outside the barn. Farmer Woodbridge walked past just as she was deciding where everyone should stand.

"Could Farmer Woodbridge take a picture with you in it, too, Mrs. Todd?" asked Peter Foster.

Mrs. Todd glanced at the farmer, and he nodded. "I'll just wash my hands first," he said.

"All right," said Mrs. Todd when the farmer had hurried off. "I'll take the first picture while we're waiting."

She finished arranging the class the way she wanted them and told them to stand still. Just then, a loud bleating filled the air.

"That's Snowy!" said Mandy. "I guess she's hungry."

"No!" cried Dillon. "She sounds frightened. I think something's wrong." Before anyone could stop him, Dillon ran off in the direction of Snowy's pen.

Mandy threw a worried look at Mrs. Todd, who nodded, and Mandy went after Dillon. Behind her, she heard a murmur of voices and someone shouting for Farmer Woodbridge. Then came the sound of running footsteps as her classmates started to follow her.

Mandy could see two figures inside Snowy's pen — one on the hay bale and one reaching out to pick up the little lamb. She heard Dillon shouting, "Leave Snowy alone!"

The figures turned slightly, and Mandy recognized them. It was Gary, Dillon's brother, and his friend, Martin.

Martin was holding up a bleating and struggling Snowy, while Gary was taunting the little lamb with a stick.

Mandy saw Dillon scrambling up onto the hay bale. Grabbing the stick from his brother, he shouted, "You're stupid, Gary! You're nothing but a bully. It's not right to tease something weaker and smaller than you are. You and Martin should know better. Put Snowy down!"

Farmer Woodbridge came up next to Mandy and took her arm to slow her down. "Wait," he said. "I think Dillon can handle this."

It was only a few seconds, but it felt like forever to Mandy and the others as they watched Dillon glaring fearlessly up at the bigger boys.

"Okay, Farmer Dillon. You win. Here, take the silly animal!" Martin thrust Snowy into Dillon's arms, and Mandy let out a sigh of relief.

But as Dillon was petting and calming Snowy, Gary leaped onto the hay bale and stood gazing at his brother.

"Your little brother looks like an idiot, cuddling a little lamb like that," Martin said mockingly to Gary.

But Gary didn't grin back. Instead, he moved

closer to Dillon and said firmly, "Lay off, Martin. I mean it. Dillon knows what he's doing. We're the idiots — it's just a baby."

Dillon held Snowy closer and looked doubtfully at Gary. It was clear he couldn't believe what he'd heard.

Martin obviously didn't believe Gary, either. "Well, if that's the way you feel, I'll leave you here to play farmer with your little brother!" he challenged.

Gary gazed at his onetime friend and said, "Yeah, you do that, Martin." He smiled at his little brother.

Gary helped Dillon down, and Mandy and her classmates started to cheer softly. Martin jumped off the hay bale and dashed off.

"All right," Mrs. Todd said a few seconds later. "You should all go to your own animals now. I'll come and take pictures of each pair. Before we leave we can take the one all together outside the barn."

The others went off to their animals, and Farmer Woodbridge walked over to Dillon and patted him on the back. "Good job!" he said. "If you want to work with sheep, there'll be a job here for you. I just wish you were old enough to start now," he added. Dillon put Snowy down and looked thoughtfully at Gary. Then he turned to look at Farmer Woodbridge. "My brother's looking for a job," he said.

Farmer Woodbridge replied thoughtfully,

"Maybe your brother's all right, too. I suppose he could stay a while, and we'll see how he does."

Before either Gary or Dillon had time to say anything, Snowy started running around in circles, bleating loudly.

Gary looked worried and turned to Farmer Woodbridge. "I know Martin and I were teasing her, and I'm really sorry about that," he said. "But I didn't mean to hurt her."

Farmer Woodbridge looked at Mandy and winked. They knew Snowy was bleating because she was hungry. "What do you think?" he asked.

Mandy smiled up at him. "I think all Gary needs is a few lamb lessons," she said. "Starting with helping Dillon to feed Snowy."

Mandy was still smiling as she ran to the farm kitchen to get Snowy's bottle. She knew their last day at Woodbridge Farm Park would be the one she remembered the most. And she knew that Dillon would *never* forget it!

coming soon

DOGGY DARE

by Ben M. Baglio

"Mrs. Todd, our teacher, told us all about Joey being deaf," she said. "How we have to look at him when we're talking and things like that."

Mrs. Appleyard nodded. "It's probably going to be difficult for him at school sometimes," she said. "He'll be getting an assistant soon, though, someone to help when he doesn't catch what Mrs. Todd says."

The telephone began to ring inside Joey's house, and his mom turned to answer it. "You and James are welcome to come over whenever you like," she said. "And will you tell Joey for me that his snack will be ready in ten minutes? And he's not to encourage that dog!"

Mandy promised to pass on the message. While she was talking to Joey and James, the ball they were playing with rolled into the gutter and went farther down the road.

No one paid much attention to the ball or Scruff going to get it until he was standing behind Joey with the ball in his mouth. He put it down and began to bark to attract Joey's attention. Joey, who was busy watching Mandy's lips as she was talking, still didn't realize Scruff was there.

Scruff barked on, but before Mandy or James could tell Joey about him, the little dog suddenly put out a paw and tapped Joey's foot.

Joey looked down, surprised. "Scruff!" he said. "What do you want?"

Mandy touched Joey's arm to catch his attention. "He's brought the ball back," she said.

Joey saw it and bent and ruffled the dog's fur. "Good boy!" he said. He picked up the ball. "You're a good dog, aren't you?"

A sudden thought occurred to Mandy. Startled, she looked at James, who had the same surprised expression.

"Hey," he said. "Do you think what I think?"

Mandy nodded violently. "Yes!" she said.

Joey was looking at them, puzzled. "What's going on?" he asked.

"Well," Mandy said, "I don't know how he *does* know, but I think Scruff knows that you can't hear. He started off by barking at you, and when you didn't pay any attention, he put his paw on your foot."

"Wow!" Joey said. "That's fantastic!"

"*What* a smart dog!" Mandy said.

There was a knocking from the window of Joey's house, and Mandy and James looked around. Joey followed their glance.

"Snack time!" Joey's mom mouthed. She

made gestures of eating, and then she beckoned Joey in.

Joey looked down at Scruff sitting patiently at his feet, then at Mandy.

"What are you going to do about Scruff?" Mandy asked. "Your mom said not to encourage him."

Joey bit his lip, then he grinned. "I might forget that!" he said, and all three of them laughed.

Mandy and James said good-bye and told Joey they'd see him the next day.

As James and Mandy walked down the road, James looked back. "Hey," he said, "look at Scruff!"

As they watched, Scruff squeezed under Joey's garden gate and settled himself down in the long grass by the front wall.

"I don't think Mrs. Appleyard is going to get rid of Scruff very easily," James said.

"Neither do I," said Mandy. "I think Scruff's already made up his mind where he wants to live!"

Doggy Dare

ent page